The
Tree
Of
Hope

Published and distributed by:
Voices of Future Generations International Children's Book Series
Trust for Sustainable Living
Hampstead Norreys, Berkshire, RG18 0TN, United Kingdom
Tel: +44 (0)1635 202444
Web: www.vofg.org

Special thanks to René V. Steiner for layout and graphics support:
www.steinergraphics.com.

The Voices of Future Generations International Children's Book Series:
'The Epic Eco-Inventions' by Jona David (Europe/North America), illustrated by Carol Adlam
'The Great Green Vine Invention' by Jona David (Europe/North America), illustrated by Carol Adlam
'The Tree of Hope' by Kehkashan Basu (Middle East), illustrated by Karen Webb-Meek
'The Fireflies After the Typhoon' by Anna Kuo (Asia), illustrated by Siri Vinter
'The Species-Saving Time Team' by Lautaro Real (Latin America), illustrated by Dan Ungureanu
'The Sisters' Mind Connection' by Allison Lievano-Gomez (Latin America), illustrated by Oscar Pinto
'The Forward and Backward City' by Diwa Boateng (Africa), illustrated by Meryl Treatner
'The Voice of an Island' by Lupe Vaai (Pacific Islands), illustrated by Li-Wen Chu
'The Visible Girls' by Tyronah Sioni (Pacific Islands), illustrated by Kasia Nieżywińska
'The Mechanical Chess Invention' by Jona David (Europe/North America), illustrated by Dan Ungureanu

Under the patronage of
UNESCO

United Nations
Educational, Scientific and
Cultural Organization

This book is printed on recycled paper, using sustainable and low-carbon printing methods.

The
Tree
Of
Hope

Written by
Kehkashan Basu

Illustrated by
Karen Webb-Meek

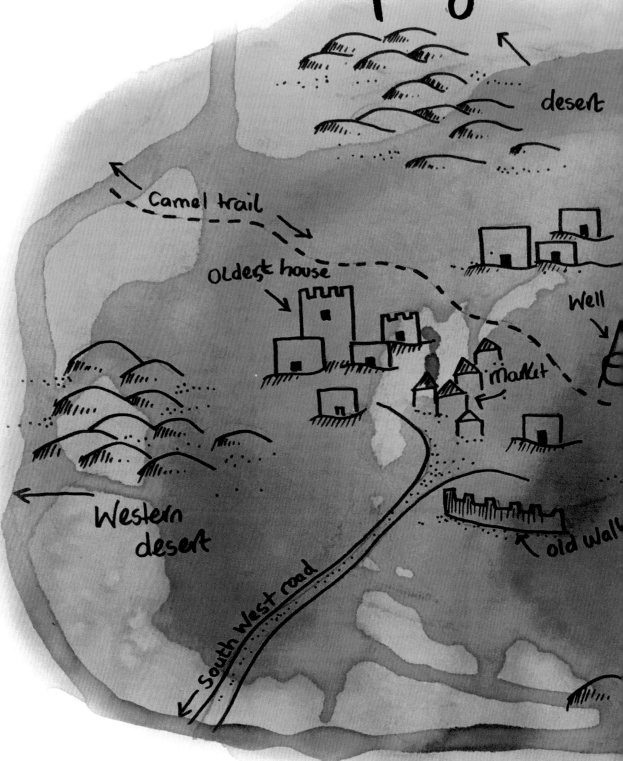

Map of the

desert

Camel trail

Oldest house

Well

market

Western desert

old Wall

South West road

ForeWord

At the World Future Council, we are dedicated to pass on a healthy planet to our children and grandchildren. As a strong voice speaking out for the rights of future generations, we are working to close the growing gap between what we should be doing, and what is being done right now. I am very happy to see that this book series is already such a success. It aims to provide a voice for you, the youth of today, and hopefully inspires you to become active yourself! Through these stories, we share two key promises that the world has made to you and to future generations: The Convention on the Rights of the Child and The Future We Want Declaration. This second book, written by our Youth Ambassador Kehkashan Basu, is an inspiring story of a girl who makes a difference, rising beyond conflict and drought, by planting and caring for trees, to benefit her whole community.

— Jakob von Uexküll
Founder and Chair, Management Board, World Future Council and
Founder of the Right Livelihood Award

Preface

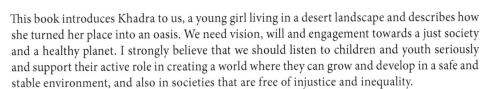

This year is crucial as world leaders will agree on a new sustainable development framework for the next 15 years during the United Nations Summit for the adoption of the post-2015 agenda. The proposed 17 goals include targets to end poverty, to ensure healthy lives and quality education and to combat climate change, among others.

This platform will be followed by a new global pact to stop climate change this December in Paris. The decisions taken will undoubtedly have a huge impact on children's lives and rights today as well as the lives and rights of future generations. Climate change is a clear violation of children's and future generations' right to life and well being.

This book introduces Khadra to us, a young girl living in a desert landscape and describes how she turned her place into an oasis. We need vision, will and engagement towards a just society and a healthy planet. I strongly believe that we should listen to children and youth seriously and support their active role in creating a world where they can grow and develop in a safe and stable environment, and also in societies that are free of injustice and inequality.

— *Maria Fernanda Espinosa*
Permanent Representative of Ecuador to the UN in Geneva,
Former Minister of Foreign Affairs, Councillor of the World Future Council

In a small village on the edge of a vast, harsh desert lived a little girl, Khadra, and her mother. The sun beat down unforgivingly on her village from early morning until night, soaking up all the moisture.

The heat was especially
unforgiving during
midday and drove
everyone indoors.

Like any other little girl, Khadra hated being cooped up inside the house and wanted desperately to play outside with her friends, but her mother would have none of it. She was afraid that Khadra would get a heat stroke if she spent the afternoon outside.

So, Khadra spent the long afternoons staring out of the window at the undulating sands which shimmered in the heat-haze and she waited for dusk so that she could go out and play.

She longed for the weather to change so that she could spend more time outdoors. She loved her home and village but wished that it was a little less hot and sunny.

Little did she realise that very soon she would have the answer to her dreams.

ne morning, Khadra was woken up early by her mother, who asked her to go to the village well to fetch water. Water was very precious in her village and the single well at the village square was its only source.

Every day, there were long queues at the well of residents waiting for a turn to haul up their daily requirement of water.

On that day, Khadra's mother asked her to go early and get some water because she was expecting a guest at their house and wanted to finish cooking in time for his arrival.

It was a chore which Khadra enjoyed as she met most of her friends at the well. She also loved the splashy sound of water and its cool, soothing feel.

The well was very deep and looked a bit scary as she peered over the parapet...

That day, she hurriedly collected the water, slung the bucket on her back and hurried back home as she, too, was excited at the prospect of meeting the guest.

Khadra did not really know who he was, except that he was her mother's distant cousin who was a traveller of sorts.

Khadra loved to listen to stories, especially of distant, exotic, faraway lands and hoped that her visiting uncle would have a tale or two for her.

Khadra's uncle finally arrived in the hot afternoon carrying a very big bag behind him.

He had a craggy but friendly face with the most twinkly eyes Khadra had ever seen. Kahra was very intrigued by him.

She couldn't wait for meal time to be over, as she wanted to hear stories of her uncle's travels.

She was also very curious to find out what was inside her uncle's heavy bag which he had placed carefully by the door.

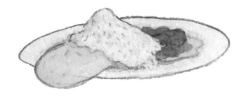

Finally, lunch was over and her mother went into the kitchen to clean up, warning Khadra to not pester her uncle and to allow her uncle to rest.

Her uncle smiled at the crestfallen look on Khadra's face and whispered to her that he wasn't really tired and would love to chat with her. Delighted, Khadra started asking him to tell her his most recent adventures.

H

er uncle said that he had recently been to another part of the world which had the most amazing forests and trees.

He described how many years ago that part of the world was also barren and dry - much like Khadra's village, but somehow the local people had found a way of changing all that.

T hey had found a plant which could grow and flourish with very little water. Every time there was a happy occasion, like a birthday or a wedding, they planted a sapling to celebrate the event..

The intention was to encourage people to plant more trees. Soon, over time, the whole area became green.

As if to prove his point, Khadra's uncle asked her to bring his bag. Telling her to be careful, he invited her to open it.

With excited fingers, Khadra untied the strings, and to her surprise it was a small sapling in a pot. The plant had very strange leaves... thick and leather-like.

er uncle said that the leaves were special and they stored water. This was the plant's speciality.

The plant was capable of storing every drop of available water from its surroundings, thus enabling it to survive long periods of drought.

Khadra's uncle said that this tree was a gift from him to her. He told her that her name meant green in Arabic and that maybe she was destined to be the person to seed her village's landscape with the colour green.

Khadra was overjoyed. This was the most exotic gift she had ever received. She gave her uncle a big hug and ran to her mother to share her excitement.

Before leaving, her uncle explained to Khadra how to plant and take care of the tree. He told her to find a place in her backyard which was in the shade and to plant it there.

He also told Khadra to save a mug of water from her bath every day and use it to water the plant. It needed very little water, he explained, as it survived on the morning dew.

As he departed, he reminded Khadra that once the tree had grown, she should collect the seeds from the plant's fruits.

He told her to give these seeds to her friends on their birthdays, and to encourage them to also plant the trees.

He hoped Khadra would take on the responsibility to live up to her name.

That evening, Khadra gathered her friends in her backyard and narrated to them the events of the afternoon.

She showed them the plant which she had been gifted by her uncle. Together they dug a hole and planted the sapling.

Time passed and Khadra's sapling flowered and grew into a large, imposing tree. Its branches and leaves offered shade during even the harshest of summers.

No longer did Khadra have to stay cooped up indoors during the afternoons. She, along with her friends, spent happy hours sitting under the tree's shade or up in its leafy branches.

Birds that had never before been seen in the village miraculously appeared and nested in the tree's branches.

Their morning songs now woke Khadra up every day.

Following her uncle's instructions, her friends plucked the tree's berries and planted the seeds in their backyards.

The village elders looked on indignantly at the children's antics, with some shaking their heads, as if to say that it was all a waste of time.

35

No one noticed at first, but it did seem as if the evenings were becoming cooler.

36

Some of the villagers even saw clouds on the horizon - something which had not been seen in many years.

The backyard of each house in the village now had one or more trees,

in various stages of bloom, each cared for by one of the children.

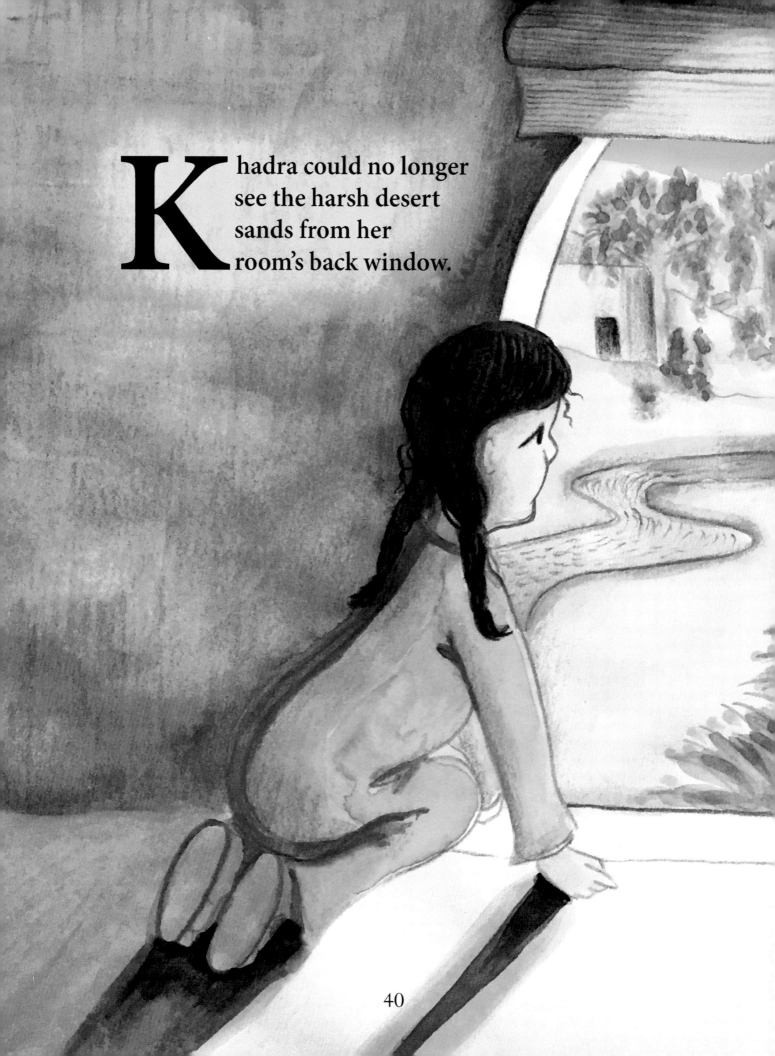

Khadra could no longer see the harsh desert sands from her room's back window.

Her tree of hope, with its lush green foliage and chirping birds, offered a beautiful green vista instead.

And finally, the unthinkable happened!

Storm clouds filled up the sky and heavy drops of rain splattered on the parched earth.

The whole village came out to feel the rain water wash away the dust and sand grains which had engulfed the villagers for so long.

42

Khadra and her friends danced in joy and drank the cool rain water until they could drink no more.

Then Khadra ran to her tree and hugged its trunk tightly to say thank you.

It had changed her village into an oasis.

It was indeed the tree of hope which had converted a barren land into a living green landscape.

The End

About the Author

Miss Kehkashan Basu

As the Youth Ambassador of the World Future Council, Kehkashan is very passionate about saving our planet for future generations, and engaging voices of children and youth in the post-2015 development agenda, which is essential for all our futures. For her, it is also important to end inequalities between girls and boys, if we want to have just societies. Thus, she is an active member of the WFC Commission on Ending Violence against Women & Girls.

Her youth organisation, GREEN HOPE, empowers young people to have a say. She conducts workshops, academies and conferences to engage and empower youth for sustainable development.

Kehkashan's advocacy on sustainability has led her to speak in over 50 international and United Nations events, carrying forward the voices of future generations. She has received awards from the UN, the Korea Green Foundation Award in 2012, the International Young Eco-Hero Award in 2013, the Kids are Heroes Award in 2014, the Solar Pioneer Award in 2015, the Ambassador for the Environment from GESS Education Awards in 2015, the Diana Award in 2015 and the prestigious NRI (Non-Resident Indian) of the Year award in 2014.

Kehkashan enjoys singing, reading, travelling, writing, painting, playing the piano and the guitar. She regularly uses art and music as mediums to spread awareness about global issues.

About the Illustrator

Karen Webb-Meek

Karen Webb-Meek lives and works on the North East Lincolnshire coast in the UK. She is married to husband Bill, an ecologist, and has four children, Katie, Poppy, Harvey and Charlie.

Karen is an avid supporter of global conservation and sustainability issues and supports the wonderful work of the WFC, UN and the other organisations lobbying for a sustainable, fair and just planet. She attended Cambridge School of Art studying for a Masters degree in Children's Book Illustration

She has worked as a professional illustrator for many years and particularly loves children's illustration and botanical illustration.

Apart from illustration, Karen is a business-woman, previously running an international swim school in 27 locations across six countries. Currently, she runs a small retail business in her home town of Cleethorpes.

Karen's favourite hobby is meeting people and chatting! She is inspired by science and discovery, and the beautiful diversity our planet offers through the natural world. She believes that sharing knowledge and education is the key to everything.

She would like to thank her husband Bill for his continuing support and encouragment in artistic pursuits, the lecturing team at Cambridge School of Art for their superb Masters degree program, and James-Lee Rudd at HoohaaDesign for his expert design input.

Voices of Future Generations Children's Book Series

Under the patronage of
UNESCO

United Nations
Educational, Scientific and
Cultural Organization

The United Nations Convention on the Rights of the Child

All children are holders of important human rights. Twenty-five years ago in 1989, over a hundred countries agreed a UN Convention on the Rights of the Child. In the most important human rights treaty in history, they promised to protect and promote all children's equal rights, which are connected and equally important.

In the 54 Articles of the Convention, countries make solemn promises to defend children's needs and dreams. They recognize the role of children in realizing their rights, being heard and involved in decisions. Especially, Article 24 and Article 27 defend children's rights to safe drinking water, good food, a clean and safe environment, health, quality of life. And Article 29 recognizes children's rights to education that develops personality, talents and potential, respecting human rights and the natural environment.

— *Dr. Alexandra Wandel*
World Future Council

Voices of Future Generations Children's Book Series

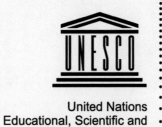

United Nations
Educational, Scientific and
Cultural Organization

Under the patronage of
UNESCO

The UN Sustainable Development Goals

At the United Nations Rio+20 Conference on Sustainable Development in 2012, governments and people came together to find pathways for a safer, more fair, and greener world for all. Everyone agreed to take new action to end poverty, stop environmental problems, and build bridges to a more just future. In 283 paragraphs of *The Future We Want* Declaration, countries committed to defend human rights, steward resources, fight climate change and pollution, protect animals, plants and biodiversity, and look after oceans, mountains, wetlands and other special places.

In the United Nations, countries are committing to 17 new Sustainable Development Goals for the whole world, with targets for real actions on the ground. Clubs, governments, firms, schools and children have started over a thousand partnerships, and mobilized billions, to deliver. The future we want exists in the hearts and minds of our generation, and in the hands of us all.

— *Vuyelwa Kuuya*
Centre for International Sustainable Development Law (CISDL)

51

Voices of Future Generations Children's Book Series

United Nations
Educational, Scientific and
Cultural Organization

Under the patronage of
UNESCO

Thanks and Inspiring Resources

'Voices of Future Generations' International Commission
Warmest thanks to the International Commission, launched in 2014 by His Excellency Judge CG Weeramantry, UNESCO Peace Education Research Award Laureate, which supports, guides and profiles this new series of Children's Books Series, including Ms Alexandra Wandel (WFC), Dr Marie-Claire Cordonier Segger (CISDL), Dr Kristiann Allen (New Zealand), Ms Irina Bokova (UNESCO), Mr Karl Hansen (Trust for Sustainable Living), Ms Emma Hopkin (UK), Dr Ying-Shih Hsieh (EQPF), Dr Maria Leichner-Reynal (Uruguay), Ms Melinda Manuel (PNG), Ms Julia Marton-Lefevre (IUCN), Dr James Moody (Australia), Ms Anna Oposa (The Philippines), Professor Kirsten Sandberg (UN CRC Chair), Ms Patricia Chaves (UN DSD), Dr Marcel Szabo (Hungary), Dr Christina Voigt (Norway), Ms Gabrielle Sacconaghi-Bacon (Moore Foundation), Ms Marcela Orvañanos de Rovzar (UNICEF Mexico) and others.

The World Future Council consists of 50 eminent global changemakers from across the globe. Together, they work to pass on a healthy planet and just societies to our children and grandchildren. (www.worldfuturecouncil.org)

United Nations Education, Science and Culture Organization (UNESCO) which celebrates its 70th Anniversary throughout 2015, strives to build networks among nations that enable humanity's moral and intellectual solidarity by mobilizing for education, building intercultural understanding, pursuing scientific cooperation, and protecting freedom of expression. (en.unesco.org)

The **United Nations Committee on the Rights of the Child (CRC)** is the body of 18 independent experts that monitors implementation of the Convention on the Rights of the Child, and its three Optional Protocols, by its State parties. (www.ohchr.org)

United Nations Environment Programme (UNEP) provides leadership and encourages partnership in caring for the environment by inspiring, informing, and enabling nations and peoples to improve their quality of life without compromising that of future generations. (www.unep.org)

International Union for the Conservation of Nature (IUCN) envisions a just world that values and conserves nature, working to conserve the integrity and diversity of nature and to ensure that any use of natural resources is equitable and ecologically sustainable. (www.iucn.org)

Centre for International Sustainable Development Law (CISDL) supports understanding, development and implementation of law for sustainable development by leading legal research through scholarship and dialogue, and facilitating legal education through teaching and capacity-building. (www.cisdl.org)

Trust for Sustainable Living and its Living Rainforest Centre exist to further the understanding of sustainable living in the United Kingdom and abroad through high-quality education. (www.livingrainforest.org)

Environmental Quality Protection Foundation (EQPF) established in 1984 is the premier ENGO in Taiwan. Implementing environmental education, tree plantation, and international participation through coordinating transdisciplinarity resources to push forward environmental and sustainable development in our time.

Voices of Future Generations Children's Book Series

Under the patronage of
UNESCO

United Nations
Educational, Scientific and
Cultural Organization

About the 'Voices of Future Generations' Series

To celebrate the 25th Anniversary of the United Nations Convention on the Rights of the Child, the Voices of Future Generations Children's Book Series, led by the United Nations and a consortium of educational charities including the World Future Council (WFC), the Centre for International Sustainable Development Law (CISDL), the Environmental Quality Protection Foundation (EQPF), the Fundacion Ecos and the Trust for Sustainable Living (TSL) among others, also the Future Generations Commissioners of several countries, and international leaders from the UN Division for Sustainable Development, the UN Committee on the Rights of the Child, the UN Education, Science and Culture Organisation (UNESCO), the International Union for the Conservation of Nature (IUCN), and other international organizations, has launched the new Voices of Future Generations Series of Children's Books.

Every year we feature stories from our selected group of child authors, inspired by the outcomes of the Earth Summit, the Rio+20 United Nations Conference on Sustainable Development (UNCSD) and the world's Sustainable Development Goals, and by the Convention on the Rights of the Child (CRC) itself. Our junior authors, ages 8-12, are concerned about future justice, poverty, the global environment, education and children's rights. Accompanied by illustrations, each book profiles creative, interesting and adventurous ideas for creating a just and greener future, in the context of children's interests and lives.

We aim to publish the books internationally in ten languages, raising the voices of future generations and spread their messages for a fair and sustainable tomorrow among their peers and adults, worldwide. We welcome you to join us in support of this inspiring partnership, at www.vofg.org.

"This poetic and lyrical story helps us all imagine the life of a girl in a country of the Middle East, the gift that trees and rain can bring to the desert, and the hope that each child offers us all."
Ms Shannon O'Shea
Programme Specialist, Post-2015 Development Agenda
United Nations Children's Fund (UNICEF)

"A beautiful tale, full of hope, dedication and community engagement, Kehkashan's book is an excellent inspiration for children around the world."
Professor Marie-Claire Cordonier Segger
Senior Director, Centre for International Sustainable Development Law (CISDL)
International Jurist and Author

UNESCO Voices of Future Generations | Children's Book Series 1
The Tree of Hope | 1

Voices of Future Generations Children's Book Series

UNESCO

United Nations
Educational, Scientific and
Cultural Organization

Under the patronage of
UNESCO

Made in the USA
Columbia, SC
11 February 2019